MW00946155

A MONSTER ATE MY MOM

Written by
Cassandra Cauvel Tucker

Archway Publishing books may be ordered through booksellers or by contacting:

Archway Publishing
1663 Liberty Drive
Bloomington, IN 47403
www.archwaypublishing.com
844-669-3957

Because of the dynamic nature of the Internet, any web addresses or links contained in this book may have changed since publication and may no longer be valid. The views expressed in this work are solely those of the author and do not necessarily reflect the views of the publisher, and the publisher hereby disclaims any responsibility for them.

ISBN: 978-1-6657-3364-9 (sc)
ISBN: 978-1-6657-3365-6 (hc)
ISBN: 978-1-6657-3363-2 (e)

Print information available on the last page.

Archway Publishing rev. date: 12/13/2022

This book is for my children, may you always enjoy the adventure of a fun and silly story. For my mother, thank you for starting my love of reading a good book. For my faithful teachers: Amy Lucy, Anita Proffitt, Elsa Barrow, and Dr. Joy Austin...Thank you for taking the time to encourage my love of literature and writing.

It was a morning, just like any other morning, or so I thought…

I woke up and I hurried down the stairs for breakfast. "Good morning, everyone!" I yelled cheerfully, but there was no reply. "That is strange!" I thought.

I went on my way and began to play with my little sister and our toys while we waited for breakfast. Our mom always makes the best pancakes. My sister and I love to play dress up, while our baby brother plays with his robot dinosaurs.

Usually, in the mornings mom sings, but today, there was no singing. Instead, I heard something strange. The noise I heard sounded like a growl! "Why was mom growling? She is so silly." I thought.

It was not long until mom came to the playroom to get my brother and sister. Mom picked up my brother and put him in his highchair. My sister and I followed. Today, mom gave us oatmeal and fruit. "Mom, where are the pancakes? I asked. "We do not have pancakes! We have oatmeal." She growled.

My sister and I were so confused by our mother's behavior. Something was not right.

"Mom, why are you talking like that?" I asked.
"I am not your mom!" She growled.
"Who are you?" I giggled. Mom is so silly.
"I am the monster who ate your mom! Now, I am going to eat you!" she growled.

Still in disbelief, my sister and I continued to eat our breakfast. My sister asked for a drink. Mom brought her one. Then, my mom did the silliest thing ever! She ATE my brother and then my sister!

It was so silly, maybe even crazy, but I saw it! My mom gobbled them each up in one bite. "Mom! What are you doing?" I squealed. Mom smiled and said: "Your sister and brother were so tasty." Then she moved closer and scooped me up! Right as she opened her mouth to swallow me, I closed my eyes and screamed!

14

15

When I opened my eyes, I was in my bed, wide awake!
What a crazy dream I just had!

I carefully, but quickly went down the stairs.

Mom was singing. "Good morning, honey! How did you sleep?" She asked.

I ran over to my mom, "oh mom! Is it really you?" I asked. "Of course it is, honey. Who else would I be?" She asked as she gave me a big hug!

And then, together with my sister, we ate our pancakes.

The End.

Cassandra Cauvel Tucker is an old soul, a daughter, a sister, a mother, and a wife. Her parents were the first to nurture her deep love of reading. As a child, Cassandra would write stories for her sister and brother. They were her first (and only) audience. Once Cassandra had children of her own, she began telling them stories. After a while, she started writing them down.